This book belongs to:

. . . .

SIMON SPOTLIGHT
An imprint of Simon & Schuster Children's Publishing Division
1230 Avenue of the Americas
New York, New York 10020

Designed and produced by Les Livres du Dragon d'Or

Adapted from the animated television series *The Busy World of Richard Scarry,*
produced by Paramount Pictures Corporation and Cinar.

SIMON SPOTLIGHT and colophon are registered trademarks of Simon & Schuster.

Manufactured in Italy

First Edition   10 9 8 7 6 5 4 3 2 1

ISBN 0-689-83490-X

The Busy World of Richard Scarry™

Richard Scarry's Best Holiday Books Ever

Santa Needs Help!

Simon Spotlight

New York   London   Toronto   Sydney   Singapore

Lowly is searching the school library for Hilda.

"There you are, Hilda!" Lowly whispers through a bookcase. "Have you chosen something to read to the class for storytime?"

"Actually, I'd like to read a story I wrote myself," Hilda replies. "I'm just worried the class might not like it."

"Don't be shy, Hilda," replies Lowly. "Reading your own story is a great idea. I can't wait to hear it! Come on!"

The class settles down around Hilda. "Ahem!" Hilda clears her throat. "My story is called *Santa Needs Help!*, by Miss Hilda Hippo."

"It was a snowy Christmas Eve in Sleepytown," Hilda begins. "Everyone was fast asleep."

"Everyone, that is, except for one very nice and very awake girl who was preparing for the most perfect Christmas ski party ever. Her name was . . . Hilda Hippo."

Sproing! Boom!
Poor Hilda! Either your skis are too long, or your doorway is too narrow.

Hilda picks up her skis and puts them by the door, to be ready for tomorrow morning.

"Wow! Just look at all that snow!" she exclaims and laughs, looking out of the window.

What Hilda was not aware of was that while all that falling snow would be great for skiing, it didn't make things easy for Santa Claus to deliver his presents that night.

"Ho, no! Why must it snow?" complains Santa.

"I wish it would melt! I wish it would go, ho, ho!"

"Here's my first stop in Sleepytown," announces Santa. "Little Bridget Murphy's house!"

"Hang on, everydeer!" calls a reindeer. "This is going to be a tough landing!"

Inside the house everyone was sleeping quietly. Little did they know what was happening on their roof!

He hurries to the window.

Boom! Crash!
"Aaah!" shouts Sergeant Murphy as he wakes up with a start. "What's that noise?"

"Hello, Sergeant Murphy," says a reindeer hanging from the roof. "Could you please help Santa fix his broken sleigh?"

Sergeant Murphy finds an unhappy Santa atop his roof.

"This is a disaster!" Santa moans. "How will I deliver all my presents with a broken runner on my sleigh? How can I fix it?"

"Fix it?" asks Sergeant Murphy. "That's it! Mr. Fixit will fix it!"

Sergeant Murphy hurries on his motorcycle to Mr. Fixit's house.
"Wake up, Mr. Fixit!" yells Sergeant Murphy. "Santa needs your help!"
Mr. Fixit is fast asleep.

Sergeant Murphy
tries to seat him
in his sidecar, but
Mr. Fixit topples in.
Boom!

Before you can say
"fix it," Mr. Fixit's
asleep again!

When they arrive at Sergeant Murphy's house, Mr. Fixit gets to work on Santa's sleigh.

"Voilà!" yawns Mr. Fixit. "Now both your sleigh runners are exactly alike."

Santa gasps in horror. "Now *both* my runners are broken!" he cries. Poor Santa!

Next door Hilda is awakened by the noise on Sergeant Murphy's roof. "What's going on?" Hilda calls from her window.

"The runners on Santa's sleigh are broken," Sergeant Murphy shouts back.

"Dear me," wonders Hilda. "If Santa can't deliver his presents then Christmas will be ruined!"

Suddenly Hilda gets an idea: "Why doesn't Santa use my *skis* as runners?"

"If I give away my skis, I won't be able to go to my ski party tomorrow," Hilda says sadly. "But there's only one thing to do," Hilda decides. "I've got to save Christmas!"

Hilda gets dressed and carries her skis to Sergeant Murphy's house. She hands them up to Santa Claus.

"Hilda, you have saved the day!" Santa says thankfully.

"Or rather, the night!" Sergeant Murphy chuckles.

"Let me nail those skis onto your sleigh, Santa!" Mr. Fixit offers.

"Thank you," replies Santa. "This time I think I'll do it myself."

My! What a busy Christmas night! Sleep tight, Hilda!

In the morning Hilda is
awakened by a knock on
her door.
"Oh, dear!" cries Hilda.
"I must have overslept!"

Hilda runs to the door.

"Merry Christmas, Hilda!"
all her friends say.
"Are you ready for the ski
party?" Lowly asks.

Poor Hilda sits down and sighs. "I can't go skiing with you," she answers. "I gave Santa my skis last night so he could fix his sleigh."

"And what did Santa give *you*?" Lowly asks.

"Gee, I don't know!" Hilda replies. "Let's look!"

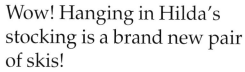
Wow! Hanging in Hilda's stocking is a brand new pair of skis!

"This is the best Christmas present ever!" Hilda exclaims, hugging her skis.

"Come on, Hilda!" Lowly says. "Now that you're all set, the ski party can begin!"

Hilda is all set to go . . .

until she realizes she still has to get dressed!

"And that's the end of my story!" Hilda tells the class.
"Bravo, Hilda!" everybody shouts as they clap.
"You know, Hilda," Lowly says, "I think that was the *best* Christmas story ever!"

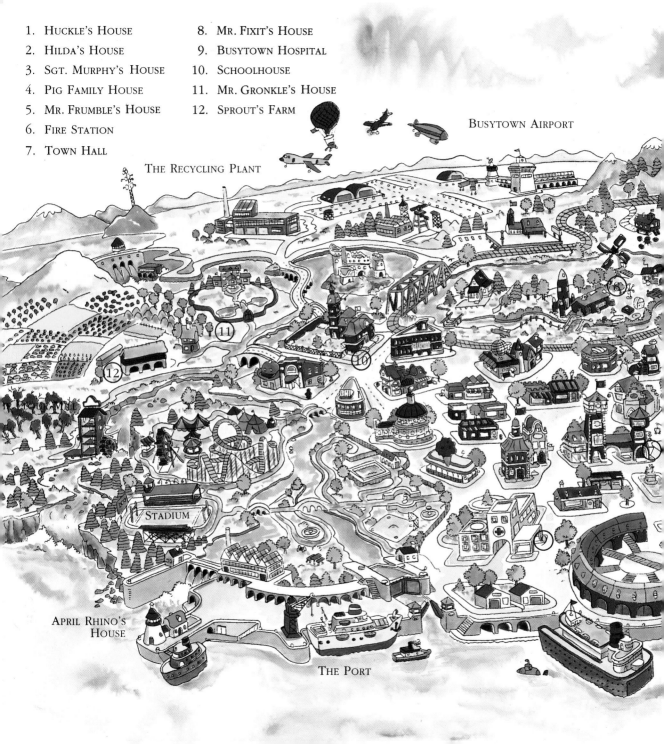

1. HUCKLE'S HOUSE
2. HILDA'S HOUSE
3. SGT. MURPHY'S HOUSE
4. PIG FAMILY HOUSE
5. MR. FRUMBLE'S HOUSE
6. FIRE STATION
7. TOWN HALL
8. MR. FIXIT'S HOUSE
9. BUSYTOWN HOSPITAL
10. SCHOOLHOUSE
11. MR. GRONKLE'S HOUSE
12. SPROUT'S FARM

THE RECYCLING PLANT

BUSYTOWN AIRPORT

STADIUM

APRIL RHINO'S HOUSE

THE PORT